9/96

VAMPIRE BUGS

Stories Conjured from the Past

Also by Sharon Dennis Wyeth

THE WORLD OF DAUGHTER McGUIRE

VAMPIRE BUGS

Stories Conjured from the Past

SHARON DENNIS WYETH

Illustrated by Curtis E. James

Delacorte Press

Published by
Delacorte Press
Bantam Doubleday Dell Publishing Group, Inc.
1540 Broadway
New York, New York 10036

LIBRARY OF CONGRESS CATALOGING IN PUBLICATION DATA

Wyeth, Sharon Dennis.
Vampire bugs: stories conjured from the past / by Sharon Dennis Wyeth; illustrated by
Curtis E. James.
p.   cm.
Includes bibliographical references.
Contents: Author's note—Vampire bugs—Little Mose—The voodoo queen—Ghost dancer
—Tale of the golden ball—Akiba's singing water.
ISBN 0-385-32082-5
1. Supernatural—Juvenile fiction.   2. Afro-Americans—Juvenile fiction.   3. Children's
stories, American. [1. Supernatural—Fiction.   2. Afro-Americans—Fiction.   3. Short
stories.]   I. Title.
PZ7.W9746Vo   1995
[Fic]—dc20   94-20315   CIP   AC

Book design by Patrice Sheridan

Manufactured in the United States of America
February 1995
10 9 8 7 6 5 4 3 2 1

For Georgia Sims Wyeth,
who listened with honest ears

Acknowledgments

M any thanks to my editor, Michelle Poploff, for her immediate response to this project and her steady support, to my friend Mary Pope Osborne for a generous push in the right direction, and to my agent, Robin Rue, for her encouragement; to the staff of the Schomburg Center for Research in Black Culture, especially to librarian Genette McLaurin; to the staff of the Wertheim Study of the New York Public Library; to the Coastal Georgia Historical Society Museum of Coastal History, Assistant Director Pat Morris; to Jessica Travis of The Historic New Orleans Collection; to Gerald and Tasallah Okona and to Geoffrey Unje for helping me with my research for "Akiba's Singing Water"; to Judy Gitenstein and Nancy Eisenbarth for their research assistance for "Ghost Dancer"; to storyteller Margaret Holtz and psychologist Thelma Markowitz for sharing their perspectives on "Tale of the Golden Ball"; and to Margaret Pine for lending me the materials she has collected on the life of Marie Laveau.

Contents

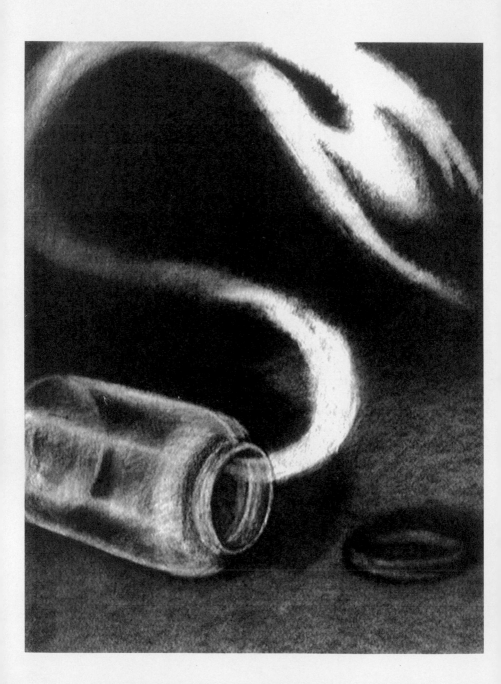

Author's Note

W ho has not been afraid in the dark of some presence felt but unseen? Of some sound heard, yet unexplained? Witches, ghosts, hags—our culture abounds with allusions to such otherworldly creatures. Out of the darkness, they latch onto our imaginations, leaving us fearful yet ever fascinated. On Halloween, the most timid will don the scariest mask. For in darkness there is power. Power that only the most gifted and brave are able to harness.

Among those versed in the powers of darkness were nineteenth-century voodoo queens—religious figures with huge followings—and neighborhood conjure men and conjure women with smaller clientele. People sought them out for their lucky charms, magic potions, and spiritual advice.

The stories in this collection feature such gifted practitioners, as well as an assortment of young people brave enough to encounter the unknown. In "Little Mose," a baby boy is reunited with his mother through the aid of the neighborhood conjure woman; in "Akiba's Singing

Water," an eleven-year-old girl, haunted by voices, meets a spirit and goes on a quest for knowledge; in "Ghost Dancer," a boy with a hole in his ear sees a dead man's face on the wall.

Tested by her powerful mother, young Marie must wrestle a hag in "The Voodoo Queen." A witch's children prove a match for animal conjurers in "Vampire Bugs." In "Tale of the Golden Ball," the child Omara finds the power within herself to break a conjure man's evil spell.

Entering realms out of the ordinary, their trust and courage challenged, these characters grasp the hand of darkness, so they may journey into the light.

This collection is a combination of fiction and adaptation, inspired by folk tale, legend, and history; the settings: from the old Southwest to the Georgia Sea Islands. At the end of the book, I have included notes explaining the source or inspiration for each tale.

When I was a child in Washington, D.C., I lived down the street from my church. But before I got to the church, there was a house that all of us ran by as fast as we could, tagging the gate as we flew past. It was said that a witch lived in that house. On my way to Sunday school, I could have gone around the other way, but I liked running past the witch. Being that scared was kind of exciting. I even secretly wished she would come to the door so that I could see her face and perhaps even meet her! Maybe I'd discover that she was just a lonely old lady. Or if she was a witch, maybe she wasn't the bad kind. Maybe she was the good kind, who could use her powers to fix some things already broken in my young life. My fascination for the dark side hasn't waned. It's what led me to research and write these stories. Run with me now and tag the witch's gate. Though lovers of the sun, we are still drawn to the night!

Sharon Dennis Wyeth
Montclair, New Jersey

Vampire Bugs

Once there was a witcher woman who could catch lightning and ride it across the sky. She lived in a hole dug in the side of a creek bank. The door of her house was covered with fresh, green tree limbs and not a soul even knew she was living there. Not even the owls or bats could keep up with this witch's comings and goings. When the moon was out, she stayed indoors, haunting the forest only on nights when the sky was black as a stack of black cats. Slipping through the woods quicker than wind, she needed no light to see by. For at will, she could gleam all over, shining from toenail to topknot—as if she were made of all fire!

Now this witcher woman had a passel of children. Just like the witch, they could make themselves gleam. The forest blinked at the sight of their lights as they whirled through the trees. Her offspring were fine to look at! But that witch was no kind of mother. Instead of feeding those young'uns milk and greens, she kept them on a diet of fresh deer blood!

On nights when the sky was black, with her children

behind her, the witch would set out into the woods to find supper. Spying some helpless buck or doe in a clearing, she would circle the animal three times, then hurl herself at the creature's eyes, while shining her topknot. Blinded by the light of the blazing topknot, the deer would stand frozen. Then the witch would mutter some magic words and the animal would become permanently paralyzed. She'd then make a high whistle and cry, "Come and eat, my children!"

The witch's little children would run out of the trees. Then the whole family would throw themselves onto the deer and begin sucking like vampires. When they were finished, there was nothing but a carcass.

The witch's children grew and grew. And so did their appetites. In order to feed them, the witch was forced to hunt by moonlight. Though deer was still their favorite, the family sucked the blood of squirrel, skunk, badger, possum, and fox. They even took a liking to bird. The floor of the forest was strewn with carcasses. The animal population was being wiped out.

Gray Fox, Badger, and Blue Jay had seen the old witch. They'd seen her hunting by the light of the moon.

"We've got to do something!" said Gray Fox.

"It's got to be quick," said Badger, "or our own tails will be turned into sausage meat!"

"We'll find a way to stop that old witch," said Blue Jay, "or I'm not the meanest bird in the forest."

Fox, Badger, and Jay hid out in a cave. All three of them knew something about conjuring—that is to say, magic spells and potions and such. They put their heads together and came up with a recipe. The recipe for a magic doe. They used dust and fish guts and all kinds of weeds; the skin and the eyes of dead deer, the seeds of wild pepper, and the perfume of flowers. Working night and day on their creation, they labored to push it out of the cave. The magic doe was life-size and lifelike. In every detail, perfect-looking! But her flesh was poison.

"Yum, yum," Jay said with a sly look in his eye.

"We did a good job," declared Badger.

"Even smells good," said Fox, taking a sniff. "Now all we have to do is go back into the cave and wait."

Darkness fell. The witcher woman sniffed out the doe and came to the clearing.

"Ain't she the prettiest!" she cackled with her mouth watering. She circled the magic doe three times around quick. Then she came up bold and shined her topknot. She muttered the magic words under her breath: "Peeph, puff, teeth, tongue. Evil rof doolb."

The magic doe didn't move, because it couldn't. But the witch thought that her magic words had paralyzed it. She licked her lips. "This doe is well fed," she said. "Maybe I'll just take a taste, before I call the children." She hurled herself on the deer's neck and started sucking. Out of sight in the cave, Jay, Fox, and Badger were watching.

At her first taste of the magic doe, the witch let out a horrible scream. Blood, flames, and smoke were spewing everywhere.

"I've been poisoned!" she screeched.

"That ain't all!" Jay laughed, sticking his head out of the cave.

The witcher woman's body began to twitch all over. Her arms flung themselves around her chest and her head hit her knees. Her toenail touched her topknot, then her legs wrapped themselves around her neck. "What's happening to me?" she yelled in terror. The old woman's body began to change shapes on her. Her body doubled and curled over and over until she was a perfect ball shape!

Then she began to shrivel.

Fox whistled. "That formula is working."

The witcher woman shrank to a quarter her size.

"Tiniest woman I've ever seen," Jay chattered.

Just then from out of the forest, they heard the children. "Mama! Where are you?" cried one of her sons.

"I'm here! By the deer!" the witch screeched.

By now, she was the size of a pig.

"I don't see her," said one of the witch's daughters.

"Mama! Mama!" cried the witch's youngest child. "I want my mama!"

"Mama! Mama!" all the others cried.

"I'm here!" the witch said in a whisper. Her voice had lost its power and she was the size of a frog. The children bumped around, trying to find her, blinking their topknots on and off.

The witcher woman shrank to the size of a charm.

Then to a pea.

Then . . . nothing!

"Good-bye, old witch!" Fox cried.

"Yes, good riddance," said Badger, "but what about the children?"

The witcher woman's children had discovered the magic doe and were eating their supper.

"Disgusting!" cried one of the witch's sons.

"I've been poisoned!" yelled one of her daughters.

"Where's my mama?" cried the youngest. "I want my mama!"

The whole crew began to cry and shrink at once.

"What a sorry sight," said Gray Fox.

"They're only children," said Badger.

Blue Jay chattered with laughter. "They won't be children for long," he said. "They're shrinking just like their mother."

The witcher woman's children were the size of pigs. They shrank to the size of frogs and then of charms.

Blue Jay kept on laughing. "Good-bye, you little bloodsuckers!"

But out of the night sky, a bolt of lightning shot through the forest. The lightning came clear through the trees and hit the forest floor. Fox, Jay, and Badger ducked out of the way, as the witcher woman's children hopped on board! The tiny little children were riding lightning!

"I never saw such. . . ," said Fox.

"Guess their mother taught them something besides bloodsucking," said Badger.

"They're getting away!" cried Jay.

The lightning rose into the sky and the children kept riding. They stopped shrinking and sprouted little wings. And when the lightning disappeared, the children kept flying. Tiny gleaming points in the dark sky.

Fox, Badger, and Jay looked up.

"Well, they're harmless now," said Fox.

"But all alone," said Badger. "I reckon they'll wonder what happened to their mama."

"Oh, nothing's left of that old lady," said Jay. "No blood, no bone. Not even the string of her petticoat."

But the witcher woman's young'uns still miss her. When the sky is as black as a stack of black cats, you can see the witch's children wandering the fields. Lightnin' bugs. Little fire children, looking for their mama.

Little Mose

L ittle Mose was only two years old when Colonel Pendleton fell in love with June Bug. June Bug was a
race horse. Little Mose was a boy who lived on Colonel Pendleton's plantation.

Down the hill from the colonel's big house, Mose
lived in a cabin. Mose lived with his mother, Rebecca.
Rebecca loved Mose and took good care of him. They
were everything to each other! Mose's father had been
sold off when Mose was only an infant. Little Mose was
born in slavery time.

When June Bug won the sweepstakes, Colonel Pendleton just had to have her. June Bug was the fastest
horse around. "I'll give you a thousand dollars for that
horse," Colonel said. This big man that owned June Bug
had a farm over Wilmington Road way.

"Thousand dollars ain't enough for me to part with
June Bug," said the big man from over Wilmington
Road way. "June Bug's a winner. But I would accept a
good fieldhand for her."

Mose's mother was coming in from the field. She was

strong. She picked cotton. Mose was riding on her hip and she was singing a song to him.

"That looks like a good strong hand," said the big man from over Wilmington Road way.

"You want her?" Colonel Pendleton said. "Then take her. Just leave me the horse."

"Come over here, Becky," said Colonel Pendleton. "You go on with this man. He got a farm over Wilmington Road way."

Rebecca held Mose closer. Mose listened to his mother's heart beating.

"I don't understand, sir," she said.

"I'm trading you for this here horse," Colonel Pendleton said, walking over to June Bug. "Go on and get your things, now. You and Mose are leaving today."

The big man from over Wilmington Road way put his hand up. "No, I don't want the baby."

Mose felt his mother's arms draw even tighter. He heard her breathing in his ear. "Please, sir," said Rebecca. "Mose is no trouble. I'll work just as hard, if only I can take him."

"I'll throw in the boy for free," Colonel Pendleton offered, feeling bad for a minute.

But the big man wouldn't have it. He'd take Rebecca by herself or nothing at all. And that's the way it was in the end. All because Colonel Pendleton wanted June Bug.

Mose felt his mother's good-bye kiss on his cheek. He felt her tears on his face. He watched her reach out for him as the man pulled her away. He saw her wave good-bye when she got in the wagon. He stood there without a sound—his heart was broken.

His neighbor old Aunt Nancy picked him up. "Don't worry, Mose. I'll be your mama now."

Aunt Nancy cooked good, but not as good as Rebecca. Her hugs were not as good either. She was too old to run and play with Mose. And she had no kind of singing voice.

"What's wrong with you, boy?" the old woman scolded at dinnertime. "You ain't touched a thing on your plate."

Mose just sat there. He didn't eat. He didn't play. All he did was think about his mother, Rebecca.

Aunt Nancy took Mose down the road to Aunt Peggy's house. Aunt Peggy was a conjure woman who fixed people's problems with spells and potions.

"Here's a mess of field peas," Aunt Nancy said, huffing and puffing. She dumped the peas out of her apron. "I'll give them to you. Just make this boy right. He won't eat. He won't play. He *can't* talk."

"He's thinking about his mother," said Aunt Peggy. She took Mose onto her lap, then glanced at the field peas. "That's a pretty small pile. You got to bring me more, next time you want me to work roots on somebody."

"Fine," said Aunt Nancy. "Can you help the boy?"

"Only one thing that's going to help," said Aunt Peggy, "and that's seeing his mama again."

Yes, I want to see my mama! thought Mose.

"Well, we know good and well that ain't going to

happen," said Aunt Nancy. "Mose ain't the first little boy who's had his mama taken away from him."

Mose hung his head. Aunt Peggy gave him a pat. "He's a right smart-looking boy. Want to see your mama, Mose?"

Mose nodded.

"What you planning?" Aunt Nancy asked.

"You'll see," Aunt Peggy said, heading for the back room. Hanging on to her skirt, Mose went with her. Aunt Nancy followed them in. Mose climbed on a stool and watched Aunt Peggy make powders.

"Drink this," said the conjure woman when she was finished crushing up the roots. She had stirred the powder in with some water. Mose took the cup and tasted something nasty. He screwed up his mouth and nose and hunched up his shoulders.

"You want to see your mama?" said Aunt Peggy.

Mose shook his head yes.

"Then drink it all up."

Mose did what she told him to. He felt a little twittering in his chest and his arms started flapping. His nose began to stretch and his legs shrank. And when he looked down at his chest, he saw feathers.

I a bird! thought little Mose.

"I declare!" exclaimed Aunt Nancy.

"Cutest hummingbird you ever saw!" said Aunt Peggy. She lifted the boy onto her finger. "Fly away, Mose! Just come back before dark or we'll all be in deep trouble."

Mose floated out of the window and onto the air. His

wings made a humming sound, which he loved! He flew as fast as he could over to Wilmington Road way.

Rebecca was sitting under a tree, crying. Mose circled her head. He hummed in her ear. He buzzed and dipped for his mother. He did a trick of flying backward and made her smile. Then he went with her to the field and picked cotton. Before he flew away, he brushed her cheek with his wing.

He flew back before dark and turned into a boy again.

For a few weeks, Mose ate. For a while, he played. He was so happy to have been with his mother. But after a while, Mose missed her so much that he got sad again.

"Here I come with this boy," Aunt Nancy said. She pulled Mose by the hand into Aunt Peggy's yard.

"And what else did you bring?" said Aunt Peggy.

"Don't worry," Aunt Nancy said. She tossed a basket of peaches on the porch. "Those'll make up into two nice pies."

"Rather have enough for three pies," said Aunt Peggy. "Though I do like the basket you brought them in," she hinted.

"Take the basket, too," said Aunt Nancy. "Just do something for this poor boy. He's back to not eating or playing again."

"Don't know what I can do," said Aunt Peggy, shaking her head. "He ain't going to be happy until he's back with his mother for good. And his mother ain't ever coming back here."

"Do what you did last time," Aunt Nancy suggested.

"If he sees her again, he'll be happy for a little while, leastwise."

Mose went up to Aunt Peggy. He hugged her around the knees and looked up at her eyes. Me go back! Me go back! he thought.

"Okay, pumpkin," said the conjure woman. She bent down and lifted him up. "How would you like to be a little mockingbird this time?"

Mose grinned. He went into the back room. He watched Aunt Peggy work the roots. He drank the nasty stuff and turned into a mockingbird. *Chack-chack-chack!* he cried. He loved his voice! He flew as fast as he could over to Wilmington Road way.

This time it was evening. Rebecca was standing in her doorway, looking up at the moon. There were tears on her face. She wiped her eyes with a handkerchief. Mose perched on a tree branch above her. He sang the melody of one of the songs she used to sing to him. Rebecca looked at him and her whole face lit up. Mose sang louder and sweeter. Then Rebecca sang a song herself and Mose sang back. Then he flew off of the tree and sat on her shoulder. She took him into the house and gave him a piece of bread from her hand.

"Sweet bird," Rebecca whispered. "If only my little Mose were a bird like you. Then he could fly away and be with me."

Mose wanted to say who he was, but could only sing or make bird sounds.

"Sweet bird," Rebecca whispered again. "I think I'm going to die."

Mose brushed his mother's cheek with his wing and flew away to Aunt Peggy's. The conjure woman had told him to be back before sunrise.

The roots wore off and Mose looked like a boy again. He sat down on the floor and cried and cried.

"First time he's crying," Aunt Nancy said. Aunt Nancy had come to fetch Mose.

"Not going to send him again," Aunt Peggy said, wagging her head. "Just tortures him, to see his mother and not be able to stay with her."

"No!" Mose cried.

The two old women looked at each other. They rushed over to Mose and bent down.

"I could have sworn he said something," said Aunt Peggy.

"He doesn't talk yet," said Aunt Nancy.

"No!" Mose said again.

"Well, he's talking now," Aunt Peggy said, getting up off the floor.

Aunt Nancy lifted him up. "What you trying to say, sugar pie?"

Mose sniffed and wiped his eyes. "Mama gonna die," he said in a small voice.

Tears came to Aunt Nancy's eyes. "His mama's going to die if she can't be with him."

"I'm sick and tired of this!" Aunt Peggy said, wiping her own tears away. "I'm putting an end to this heartache."

"What you going to do?" Aunt Nancy asked, putting Mose on the floor.

"Don't ask questions," said Aunt Peggy. "I'm mad now!"

She whipped into the back room and took some roots off the shelf. She started pounding up some powders. Mose and Aunt Nancy crept in quietly.

"Here!" Aunt Peggy said, turning to Mose. She stuck a glass of nasty stuff under his nose.

"Thought you weren't going to send him back," Aunt Nancy reminded her.

"Just one last time," Aunt Peggy said, breathing hard. She grabbed Mose by the shoulder. "Okay, Mose. Drink this up and you're going to turn into a sparrow. I want you to take a little bag tied with string over to Wilmington Road way."

"Yes, ma'am," Mose said, nodding.

"Drop it at your mother's door and fly right back," said Aunt Peggy. "When she sees this little bag, she'll think that somebody's trying to work some evil on her."

"What good will that do?" Aunt Nancy asked.

"That'll be the last straw," said Aunt Peggy. "If Rebecca thinks somebody's working some kind of evil spell on her, she'll take to her bed. The worst thing that could happen to her is to be apart from Mose. And that's already happened. If Rebecca thinks something else bad is going to happen, she'll just lie down in her bed and never get up again."

Aunt Nancy scratched her nose. "I hope you know what you're talking about."

"I do know what I'm talking about!" Aunt Peggy snapped at her.

Once more Mose drank the nasty stuff. He turned into a sparrow and picked up the funny-looking little bag in his beak. He flew over to Wilmington Road way and dropped the little bag at his mother's door. Before he left, he sang a little sparrow song that sounded like *put on your tea-kettle-ettle-ettle!*" Then he flew right back to Aunt Peggy's cottage again.

"Good work!" said Aunt Peggy. The conjure woman turned to Aunt Nancy and pointed her finger. "Now—you! Since you started all this, you might as well help out."

Aunt Nancy backed up to the window. "What you talking about?"

"Drink this," Aunt Peggy said, shoving a cup under her nose.

"What if I don't want to?" Aunt Nancy said.

"This boy has turned himself into a hummingbird, a mockingbird, and a sparrow," declared Aunt Peggy. "And all because you brought him to me. Least you can do is to turn yourself into a hornet!"

"A hornet!" exclaimed Aunt Nancy.

Aunt Peggy smiled at Mose and Mose giggled.

"Yes, a hornet," said Aunt Peggy, making Aunt Nancy drink the nasty stuff up. "Fly out to the stable and sting that old June Bug. Sting that horse right in the knees!"

Mose watched Aunt Nancy fly out of the window. He heard June Bug howling inside the stable.

That's how Mose and Rebecca got back together again:

When Colonel Pendleton saw June Bug's knees all swollen up, he fell out of love with her. And when that big man over Wilmington Road way saw how Mose's mother was just lying in the bed and wouldn't get up . . . well, they figured they'd trade back again.

"Give me back my horse!" the big man said. He'd brought Rebecca over. She was lying down in the wagon.

"Take your old lame horse!" Colonel Pendleton shouted. "Give me back my fieldhand!"

When Rebecca saw Mose, she flew out of that wagon. She was so happy, she forgot about that little bag at the door that meant somebody was trying to work evil on her. When Aunt Peggy and Aunt Nancy told her the whole story, she was ever so grateful to them.

Rebecca was also mighty surprised that Mose was talking. But she wasn't surprised at his pretty singing voice. After all, he'd been singing before he could speak. In fact, Mose sang so well that people came from miles around to hear him. They gave him money when he sang, which Mose put away. When Mose grew up, he made more money at his trade as a blacksmith. He worked for Colonel Pendleton on his plantation, but Mose also hired himself out. And with that money and the money he'd earned by singing, he bought his freedom. He worked some more and bought his mother's freedom. They'd been born in slavery time, but they died free.

The Voodoo Queen

O nce there were two Maries, a mother named Marie and her young daughter to whom she'd given her name. They lived in a cottage on St. Ann Street. Mother Marie was a very grand woman. She wore elegant blue dresses, fancy turbans, and large gold earrings. She also owned a wonderful purple silk cloak. When mother Marie appeared in the streets, all heads turned to watch her. Strangers waved and followed her, crying out her name and begging her to pray for them or to tell their fortunes. Mother Marie was a queen, the voodoo queen of New Orleans.

Little Marie was the spitting image of her mother. With her own fingers, the voodoo queen had sewn her child a magnificent little blue dress with rows of pearl buttons. The girl had her mother's large dark eyes, smooth hands, and wild tresses. But little Marie had no playmates. To most of the world, the girl did not exist. Because whenever little Marie went outdoors, mother Marie turned her into a shadow.

Opening the door of their cottage, the voodoo queen

would step into the courtyard. "Come, *ma petite*!" she would call to her daughter. The child would take her mother's hand and step forward. Mother Marie would kiss her forehead. "Come into the folds of my cloak," she would say. "Today you will become my little shadow." Soothed by her mother's gentle voice and kiss, the child would step into the perfumed folds of the silk cloak and disappear.

Madame Marie stepped into the street. A tall, elegant woman in a purple cloak, with a small shadow at her side. As she hurried to work, her shoes made a clacking sound on the brick sidewalk.

"Madame Marie! Madame Marie!" one woman called out, running after her. "My fiancé no longer loves me! Please give me gris-gris!"

"Bring his glove to my house this evening," the voodoo queen instructed. "I'll fill it with steel dust and honey. You'll sleep with it. Ha, ha! Your fiancé will love you again! Never fear!"

The voodoo queen kept walking with the small shadow at her side. The woman who had asked for gris-gris had not even seen the child. When little Marie was a shadow, no one could see or hear her. But wherever little Marie went, she saw and heard everything.

Sometimes the little shadow accompanied her mother to Congo Square or Lake Pontchartrain. There she watched Madame Marie lead the great dances. And with her mother, little Marie also went to Parish Prison, where men convicted of murder waited for Madame Marie's gumbo. The gumbo which the voodoo queen prepared for the prisoners was no ordinary soup. By now little Marie knew the recipe: chicken, okra, and crawfish in a savory broth flavored with ground sassafras and thickened with flour and pork drippings—ordinary ingredients but rendered very potent by strange-smelling magic drops which the voodoo queen added to the pot from little brown bottles.

Little Marie was there when the prisoners drank the mixture. She was a shadow in the corner, hearing her mother's voice as she prayed over the men. A shadow at her mother's side, when the men were done eating and the voodoo queen left the prison. With her mother, little Marie passed through the crowd and by the gallows. She heard the people cry out the voodoo queen's name. And then she saw the prisoners in their blindfolds led forth to die.

The wind picked up. The sky grew dark. A sudden bolt of lightning split the gallows in two! The executioner fell down on his knees crossing himself. The voodoo queen and her shadow hurried away from the crowd. "It's a sign from God," little Marie heard someone say. "There will be no hanging today! Madame Marie has been to visit the prisoners!"

Little Marie felt proud of her mother. The men were innocent. Her mother had saved them.

When the two Maries returned home from such outings, the child stepped out of the cloak and became a real girl again. She gave her mother a kiss and went to play with her doll, while mother Marie made their own supper, two bowls of gumbo—but of the ordinary kind. After supper, Marie's mother would help her child bathe. Then she gave little Marie lessons in reading and sewing and taught her to make fancy curls in her hair. At night there was often a knock at the door—a customer. Mother Marie would shoo her child into the back room, where little Marie played with her doll dishes in the shadows. The child could hear her mother's voice from the front room, speaking in kindly tones to some stranger. She heard the shuffle of cards as Madame Marie predicted the caller's future and later the clink of coins on the table when the voodoo queen was paid for her work. On other nights, through the window the child spied on gatherings of the voodoo queen's followers, meetings in the backyard under the stars, with lots of lit candles and drums, where the famous queen spoke to the crowd about life's mysteries.

Marie knew her mother's work was important. She also knew that it put bread on the table. But by the age of fourteen, Marie was restless. She wanted to go outside alone. She wanted to make friends. She wanted to be seen and known—to have a life of her own.

"Come with me, *ma petite*," her mother would say. "Today you will be my little shadow."

Marie would toss her curls and look away. "No," she said. "I don't want to go with you. I want to go out on my own. And I'm not your little shadow anymore. I'm too old for that!"

Mother Marie was strict. She wasn't used to back talk. "Whatever happened to my sweet, obedient girl?"

she said. Reaching out, she tried to stroke her daughter's head.

"Don't touch me," Marie said, pulling away. "How would you like to be a prisoner? To never breathe the air outside these walls? To be smothered in your mother's cloak? To be called a shadow?"

"It isn't safe for you to go out on your own," said Marie's mother. "A girl your age . . . what would you do?"

Marie looked out of the window. "Meet people, go exciting places, perhaps to dances."

"And how would you take care of yourself?" asked her mother. "You've always had my protection."

"I don't need your protection," said Marie. "I don't need anything from you. I can work, too."

The voodoo queen looked into the mirror. She tapped her heavy gold earrings. "And just what kind of work would you do?" she asked her daughter.

Marie tossed her head. "The same kind you do," she said. "I'm sure I could do it just as well."

Her mother turned. "You aren't ready yet," she said. "And there can only be one of us."

Marie looked into her mother's face. The voodoo queen's eyes were burning coals of anger. Marie felt nervous, but she didn't back down.

"You may think I'm not ready," she said stubbornly, "but I do. Every day of my life I have been watching you. But I suppose you want to hide me under your cloak forever. I suppose you want me to die there."

"Enough!" said her mother. She pulled her silk cloak

from the peg and wrapped it around herself. "I'm going out," she said. "Since you no longer need me, you can stay here."

The door slammed. Marie hurried to the window. She saw the tail of her mother's cloak and heard the clack of Madame Marie's shoes on the brick sidewalk.

That night Marie made her own supper. She washed up and put herself to bed. When she closed her eyes, her mother had not returned.

But in the middle of the night, Marie woke up with a jolt. Something heavy and invisible sat on her chest. Marie struggled to push it off, but the terrible thing pressed harder still. "Get off!" Marie screamed. The weight was heavy as stone. But Marie knew it was no boulder on her chest, but a spirit—a hag!—who had come to ride her.

"Get off me, hag!" she screamed even louder. Marie pushed with all her might. She struggled for hours. But she couldn't push the hag off her chest. There was nothing for her to do but lie still until daylight. She knew that then the hag would become a blue vapor and float out of the window.

The next day, Marie waited for her mother. Madame Marie knew all about hags. People had often come to ask the voodoo queen how to get rid of them. When her mother came back, no hag would dare to haunt her, thought Marie. But no purple cloak appeared in the distance. No sound of clacking heels in the street. And when twilight came, the voodoo queen still wasn't back.

Marie worried about her mother and worried about herself. She sat in a corner, afraid to go to bed.

"Please, come back, Mama," she whispered.

Darkness fell. Marie lit a candle. She sat on a chair by the window and began to read a book. Perhaps if she stayed awake, the hag wouldn't come back again.

But soon enough Marie's eyes grew heavy. The breeze blew out the candle and the book fell to the floor. When Marie awoke with a jolt, she too was on the floor—pinned down by the weight of ten boulders!

"Get off, hag!" she screamed. She wrestled with the spirit. She kicked with all her strength. For a moment, it felt as if she might push the hag off. But in the end, the spirit was stronger and Marie had to surrender. Scarcely able to breathe, she lay on the floor until dawn, when the hag became a blue vapor and floated away.

Marie got up, exhausted. She dragged herself to the kitchen to fix breakfast. How she wished that Madame Marie were there to keep her company. She missed her mother's kiss and laugh. She missed the hustle bustle in the cottage as the voodoo queen dressed for work. But most of all, Marie missed her mother's protection. She waited by the window, but in vain. By late afternoon, when it seemed that her mother would not return, Marie hurried to find Madame Marie's sewing basket. She knew what she had to do.

From the basket of the voodoo queen, young Marie took nine new needles. She took a jug from a high shelf and filled it half full with spring water. She found a new cork in the drawer and one by one she stuck the new needles into one end of it. Marie hung the bottle with water on the outer post of her bed, close to the headboard. And at sundown, she hung the cork just an inch above the bottle and got into bed. If the hag came back that night, Marie would be ready.

The spirit did come. It sat on Marie's chest. Marie let the spirit ride her without a struggle. And at daybreak, as the weight of the spirit lifted, Marie reached over the top of her head. The invisible hag had become a blue vapor. Marie caught it by the tail as it was floating away. Then she quickly stuffed the spirit into the bottle! Then with the nine-needle cork, she stopped up the bottle's opening.

"I've got you!" Marie cried. "You won't be bothering me anymore, you old hag!"

The vaporous shape inside of the bottle turned and twisted. It butted itself against needles and churned the water. Pressing her palm against the smooth end of the cork, Marie made sure that the stopper was tight. Then she placed the bottle on a shelf, cleaned the house, made tea, and waited for her mother.

The sun was setting when mother Marie appeared at the gate. Instantly Marie saw that something terrible had happened. Her mother's cloak was faded and tattered. Her steps were slow. And her shoes made no clacking sound.

"Mama!" Marie cried, running into the courtyard. "Did someone rob you? Why were you gone so long?"

"Never mind," mother Marie said in a soft voice. She

touched her daughter's head. "How is my brave, strong girl?"

Marie hugged her mother. "I'm fine, but I missed you, Mama. I'm sorry I was so rude to you."

The mother put a finger to her lips. *"Sh,"* she said, "it's all over now."

The two Maries walked into the cottage. Marie noticed that her mother's face was badly scratched and that the bottom half of her elegant blue dress was waterstained. Madame Marie sat down at the table and rested her head in her hands.

"How tired you look, Mama," said Marie. "I'll make tea for you."

"Thank you, *ma chérie,*" said the mother.

As Marie hurried to fetch the hot kettle, the voodoo queen loosened her turban. In the few days that she'd been gone, her raven-dark hair had become streaked with white.

Marie drew in a breath. "How white your hair has become," she exclaimed.

The voodoo queen sighed. "It happens to everyone."

Marie brought the tea and set it in front of her mother. Sitting at the table, her mother seemed so small. "How bowed your back is, Mama," said Marie.

The voodoo queen sipped her tea carefully. "That is what happens when one grows old."

"But you are not old!" Marie protested. "You are still a young woman."

"Hush," said mother Marie, "there is little enough time in the world. Let's not spend it chattering about me. Tell me about yourself—when I was away, how did you manage?"

Marie grinned. "At first I was very scared," she confessed. "A hag came to visit and was riding me. But I caught her all by myself!" She went to the shelf and took down the bottle. "I've got her spirit—see!"

The voodoo queen nodded slowly.

Marie peered at the twisting blue vapor. "Whoever sent their spirit to haunt me is being punished. Everyone knows that once a person's spirit is captured, that person will die."

The voodoo queen nodded and closed her eyes.

Marie put the bottle down and rushed to her mother. "Poor Mama," she said, "you are exhausted. Would you like me to put you to bed?"

Mother Marie opened her eyes a bit. "No, I'll sit here a little longer." She stroked Marie's smooth hand. "You have learned a good lesson while I was gone. How to use your wits as well as your strength. I now have no doubt that you can take care of yourself."

"But I won't have to take care of myself," said Marie. "I'll still have you to take care of me. You won't be going away again, will you?"

The voodoo queen fingered one of her gold earrings. "I will be leaving again," she said, "but this time I'll be away much longer."

Marie grabbed her mother's hand. "No," she begged, "please don't go. I missed you so much while you were gone. And another hag might come to visit me in the night."

Mother Marie smiled. "And you'll catch her spirit in a bottle," she said, "just like you did this time." She patted Marie's hand. "I didn't know you were so strong. You gave that old hag a good fight. She came back three times. But on the third night you were ready for her."

"How do you know the hag came for three nights?" Marie asked. "You weren't here."

The voodoo queen stirred her tea. "You might as well know," she said. "I was here."

"Where?" asked Marie in surprise.

"I was the hag," her mother confessed. "I came to punish you and then returned to test your strength. You have my spirit there in the bottle."

"No!" Marie cried. "It can't be! That means that you are going to die!"

Mother Marie gave her a stern look. "We all die. My mission in life was to take care of you. Now that you are grown, my mission is over."

Marie began to wring her hands and cry. "No," she said, "I'll unstop the bottle. I can't kill my own mother!"

The voodoo queen's eyes narrowed. "Even though I turned you into a shadow?"

Marie got down on her knees. "I admit I wanted my freedom. I was also ambitious. I thought that I should be a queen too." She wiped her eyes and kissed her mother's smooth hands. "But nothing is worth your death, Mama."

"I turned you into a shadow in order to protect you," said mother Marie. "But I see that I was smothering you as well."

"I forgive you for that," said Marie. "I will be a shadow for the rest of my life, if you only teach me how to save you."

"Stand up," her mother commanded. "Not only have you strength and wit, but the power that comes from forgiveness. Now, help me stand."

Marie stood up and then helped her mother. The voodoo queen was so weak, she held on to the chair. "Take the bottle," she instructed.

Marie took the bottle from the table. The blue vapor inside had grown quiet.

"Now, take my cloak," said mother Marie, "and wrap it around you." Marie did as she was told.

"Go to the cemetery," the queen instructed. "Take my spirit with you and speak to no one. Dig a chunk of earth from behind the farthest marker and tie it into the corner of your handkerchief. If you truly wish me to live, pray for it with all your heart. Then open the bottle."

Tears streamed down Marie's face. She looked at her mother and then at the vapor in the bottle. The blue color of the spirit seemed to be fading.

"What if I'm too late?" the daughter asked.

"If that be the case, when you come home, you will find my body. Get the priest for my funeral." Then she smiled. She looked almost like the old Marie again. "But if you manage to save my life," she added, "I'll be having a dinner party. Today is St. John's Eve, you know."

Marie nodded.

"When you return," mother Marie said, "look into the window. If I am alive, come in the back way. Your clothes will be laid out on the bed. Get dressed and join the dinner guests."

Marie smiled. "I don't have to hide in the back room?"

"No," her mother said gently. "But you must only join the party when the clock strikes eleven. Take the eleventh empty chair when you enter the room. And my friend Doctor John will make a toast meant especially for you."

The voodoo queen sank into her chair. "Now, hurry!" she whispered.

Marie kissed her mother good-bye. With the bottle tucked under the purple silk cloak, she rushed out of the cottage and onto St. Ann Street. She heard the clack of her own heels on the brick sidewalk as she made her way. She felt the breeze on her face. Her heart pounded loudly. It was the first time she'd been out in the world on her own! Passing Congo Square, she heard a man's voice cry out, "Madame Marie! Madame Marie!" Someone had mistaken her for her mother! Marie longed to stop and talk. She wanted to explain. But her mother's instructions had been to speak to no one. As the beautiful young woman in the purple cloak wound her way through the crowded streets, people's heads turned. Some smiled at her or waved and called out. But young Marie kept her eyes straight in front of her. The only thought she had on her mind was to reach the cemetery.

With the bottle clutched to her chest, she hurried to the final marker. She got down on her knees and dug out a clump of earth, which she tied into the corner of her

handkerchief. Then, pulling the nine-needle cork out of the bottle, she prayed:

"Let my mother live! Let my mother live!"

The thin, blue cloud in the bottle slowly slipped away, vanishing into the air. Young Marie stood up. Then, clutching the clod of earth in her handkerchief, she ran all the way back home to St. Ann Street.

One peek at the front window told Marie that all was well. Her mother was alive and entertaining her guests. Marie sighed with relief. Mother Marie didn't appear tired at all and had never looked more beautiful. Keeping out of sight, young Marie obediently slipped in the back way.

On the bed, new clothes were waiting: a bright-colored turban, gold earrings, an elegant blue dress. There was even a shimmering new purple silk cloak. Marie tossed off the old cloak she had been wearing and quickly got dressed. Tonight was the very first time she had been invited into the front room when her mother had guests! As she slipped into her new blue dress, she heard the clink of forks against plates as the guests ate their supper. She heard the echo of gay conversation and her mother's laughter as she wrapped the bright turban around her dark hair. She put on her gold earrings and looked at herself in the mirror. How grown-up she looked and felt! And she looked so much like her mother. . . .

The clock struck eleven and young Marie made her entrance. Ten guests stood at the table with their glasses raised. At the head of the table the eleventh empty chair waited. Marie smiled and looked around. The guests smiled back, each murmuring a good evening. Marie, who had never been known or seen by strangers, was filled with pleasure. Still smiling, she looked around for her mother. But the voodoo queen wasn't in sight.

From the foot of the table, a man with mysterious eyes gazed at her. He clinked his glass with a knife, then cleared his throat.

"Let us drink to the health of our queen," he said in a deep voice.

Marie looked around again for her mother. Mother Marie still wasn't there. And the eyes of every guest were on young Marie.

"To the health of our queen," said the woman standing right next to her. She looked Marie straight in the face.

The mysterious man at the foot of the table let out a huge laugh. "May she never grow old!"

"Amen, Doctor John!" another voice cried. "To our queen!"

"To our queen!" the other guests shouted. Raising their glasses in Marie's direction, they drank their toast to her. Then Doctor John offered the young woman his arm.

"The carriages are waiting," he said. "Will you come with us to the lake and lead the dance?"

Marie nodded yes. Carried away by the excitement of the party, she went out with the guests. Her purple silk cloak shimmered in the moonlight. A procession of people with torches was lined up by the carriages. As she stepped onto the brick sidewalk, she heard the clack of her shoes and the crowd cried out: "Madame Marie! Madame Marie! Pray for us, Marie! Tell us our fortune!"

For many years, Marie remained queen. Sitting on a velvet couch, she received guests in the cottage on St. Ann Street. And sipping tea in the shadows was a kind-looking old woman in a faded cloak.

Voodoo—Practices containing magic and elements of an ancient African religion.

Gris-gris—Magic charm, potion, or prescribed ritual.

Congo Square—The mother and daughter in this story are "free people of color." Most African-Americans living in New Orleans prior to the Civil War were slaves. An ordinance passed in 1817 limited their right of assembly to one two-hour period every Sunday. At that time they were allowed to gather for dances in an area that became known as Congo Square.

Doctor John—Legendary voodoo priest.

Ghost Dancer

B rian Boyd was born with a ghost hole in his ear. A tiny hole in the bottom of his earlobe. A child born with a ghost hole in his ear can see ghosts. But it wasn't until Brian was nine years old that he actually did see one.

Brian was an only child. He lived with his mother, Eliza. He had never known his father, a soldier by the name of Bob Boyd. Only a few days after Brian was born, Bob Boyd had gone off with the Cavalry, never to return. "Your father was a good man," Eliza told Brian when the boy was older. "He wanted to give you honor. And he made a promise to me that he'd always take care of us. Would have kept that promise, I know," said Eliza, "if only he hadn't been shot down."

Brian listened with only half an ear to his mother's stories. If his father had wanted to take care of them so much, why wasn't he there? Where was he when the wheat crop failed? Where was he when the cough came on Eliza? Where was he when no more milk would come from the cow?

Nine years old, Brian was grown before his time, doing a man's labor in the field, helping his mother. Listening to the wind twist on the prairie.

The mother and son got by well enough, until the day Eliza's cough got so bad she couldn't get up. The sound of her racking cough went straight through the boy. Like the prairie's whine, it made him shiver. Wrapped in a quilt, Eliza sat up in bed holding Bob Boyd's picture.

"If your daddy was here," she told Brian, "he would take care of us. But he ain't. So, run along now and get Miss Red Moon. Tell her your mother's feeling poorly. Tell her to bring some of her medicine weeds."

Eliza went into one of her coughing fits and Brian stared.

"Go on, now," choked Eliza. "If anything happens to me, Miss Red Moon will take you."

Frightened, Brian bolted out of the door. In the vast emptiness of his world, Eliza had been his strength. The one he could always hold on to. The only human being he ever saw, except for their Indian neighbor, Sallie Red Moon. Plunging into the waist-high grass, he walked the three miles to Miss Red Moon's. The Lakota woman had known the Boyds since before Brian was born. She had kept friends with them even after Bob Boyd rode out against her people with the Calvary. When Brian arrived, Miss Red Moon was roasting a rabbit. Her big yellow dog stood watch at the door and barked to announce Brian's arrival.

"How," said Miss Red Moon. "What brings you here, son?"

"We got trouble," said Brian. "Ma's sick—bad sick this time."

"I'll be with you," said the woman. Miss Red Moon took the roasting meat off the spit and wrapped it, while the big yellow dog yipped and licked fresh drippings off the floor. The Lakota woman washed her hands and got her pouch. Then, leaving the door unlocked, she and Brian and the yellow dog made their way through the tall grass, back to Eliza.

That night, Brian had rabbit for supper and Eliza had Miss Red Moon's special herb tea. Thanks to the tea, Eliza's cough quieted. After sleepless nights of worrying about his mother, Brian was able to fall into a deep sleep.

But the low growl of the yellow dog soon awoke the boy. Brian rolled over in his hard pine bed. Across the room, his mother was a frail lump beneath her quilt. Wrapped in a blanket in the corner was Miss Red Moon's somewhat heftier form. And crouched by the dying fire was the growling dog. Brian glanced at the window. There was nothing out of the ordinary, only the icy form of a low-dipping moon. But on the far wall was a sight that made his skin crawl—a face! A man's face, both visible and invisible—Brian could see him and yet see through him.

Brian shut his eyes tight. The face had reminded him of someone, but he was so frightened, he couldn't think who. "Go away!" he whispered. He waved his hands blindly. "Nobody wants you! Go away!" He peeked out of one eye and then the other. The ghost had faded and the yellow dog was quiet.

The next day Eliza was better, but still kept to her bed. "I've talked to Miss Red Moon," she told Brian. "She'll keep you if I should die. Meanwhile, you must take your father's picture."

Brian took the small picture frame Eliza held out to him. A dark handsome face stared up out of the photograph, a young man with hair curly as a sheep's and a blue soldier's cap. Brian drew in a breath and tossed the picture onto the bed. It was the face he had seen on the wall!

Eliza coughed. "What's wrong with you, boy? You take good care of that. There's a letter inside the back of the frame, a letter he wrote to me."

Brian picked up the picture. "I'll take good care of it," he promised, kissing his mother's cheek.

He carried the photograph outside. Miss Red Moon sat on the stairs, smoking a pipe.

"How," she said. "Your ma is better."

"Howdy," said Brian. "Yes she is and we thank you. But things are still strange here." He looked at the picture and then looked away.

"How are they strange?" asked the woman.

Brian sat down next to her. "Last night," he whispered, "I saw a ghost!"

Miss Red Moon did not look surprised.

"Well, your ma told me that story once about the ghost hole," she said. "Me, I never heard of that. But your ma figured that you might see a ghost one day. Since you got a hole in your ear."

Brian nodded. "She told me that too. Only I was hoping that I'd never see one."

"Were you scared?" asked Miss Red Moon.

"Reckon I was," said Brian, "even though it was the ghost of my own father."

Miss Red Moon's eyes gleamed with curiosity. "Ah," said the woman, "and what did he tell you?"

"Oh, I didn't talk to him," said the boy. "I told him to go away."

"What a shame," said the woman, "he might have told you something."

"He's a ghost," said Brian. "What could he tell me?"

"Plenty," said Miss Red Moon. "When I was younger I met the ghost of my grandfather. He told things that I still remember. If your father comes again, you should welcome him."

Brian hung his head. "What if I'm afraid?"

Miss Red Moon reached into her pouch. She pulled out a small doll made of hide and hair, wearing leggings and a white cotton shirt with a painted red moon. "Take him," she said. "He is a ghost dancer doll. When your father comes again, hold on to the doll for luck."

"Thank you," said Brian, holding his hand out. The doll's worn face had no expression, but Brian thought that it looked very brave.

That night Brian lay awake with his eyes wide open. Across the room, Eliza slept soundly and Miss Red Moon slept in the corner. Tonight even the yellow dog was asleep. Again a low-dipping moon filled the far window. But no ghost appeared. Brian sat up in bed and looked at the small photograph. He remembered the letter his mother had told him about. Prying open the back of the small frame, he pulled a thin slip of paper out. By the light of the moon, he strained to read his father's faded but still elegant handwriting:

Dearest Eliza,

May we be joyful in our lives and in death may we not be parted.

Brian folded the letter carefully and put it back. Perhaps this is what the ghost of his father had wanted—to take his mother with him to the land of the dead! Brian reached inside his pocket and fingered the doll. No matter what his father wanted, he thought, this time he would welcome him. His father had died before he was born. Brian had never had a chance to talk to him. He wanted that chance, even if his father was a ghost.

The next morning, Eliza still coughed, but she was strong enough to sit by the stove. After breakfast Brian sat on the porch with Miss Red Moon.

"Your ma will be well soon," the woman told the boy.

"We're grateful for your help," said Brian.

"Did your father's ghost come back last night?" Miss Red Moon asked.

Brian shook his head. "I think I scared him away.

Now I wish I hadn't. I never got to meet my father before."

The woman lit her pipe and stroked the yellow dog. "There was a way we had," she said, "a way we had to welcome our ghosts. We wore magic shirts or blouses, painted like the doll's. We danced a special dance and sang special songs. If we were lucky, the dead came to us."

Brian took the ghost dancer doll out of his pocket. "Is that how you met your grandfather?" he asked.

The woman nodded. "The Ghost Dance was not just magic," she said, "it was a religion. We danced to see the return of the old life, the buffalo, our loved ones, and our lands. This is something I don't talk about much. But to you I can."

Brian nodded and listened. He knew well that all around had once been the land of the Lakota people. He knew that the Calvary had gone against them. Brian's father had been in the Calvary.

"My father was a Buffalo Soldier," said Brian. "He was one of those who went against your people."

"That was another time," said Miss Red Moon. "And that was them—not you and me, not us." She laid a hand on Brian's curly head. "You and me and your ma are close. If she had died, you would have been my son."

Then she took the pipe she had been smoking and gave it to the boy. Like a grown man, Brian accepted the pipe and took a puff.

"If you like," the woman said, "I will teach you the dance. Maybe the ghost of your father will come back."

"I would like that," said Brian.

"This will be a powerful night then," said Miss Red Moon. "This afternoon I will go home for a bit. Wash yourself especially well, as if you were going to town."

"I will," said Brian.

Miss Red Moon left. Brian filled the big iron tub by the stove with spring water. He washed himself well.

"Why are you bathing in the middle of the week?" asked Eliza.

"I fell in the barn," Brian replied, telling a little lie. He thought his plans to meet the ghost might alarm Eliza, weak as she was.

His mother smiled and closed her eyes. "You're a funny boy," she said. "Just see that you stay near me."

"I will," said Brian.

When Miss Red Moon returned, Eliza was asleep. The Lakota woman gave Brian a beautiful shirt. It was white with blue beads and a red painted moon and stars on it. Brian noticed that the shirt was similar to the one worn by the ghost dancer doll.

"This was my brother's," said Miss Red Moon. "Even though we were children, our elders let us dance. They knew we were brave enough to be honored. The shirt is powerful, like medicine. Put it on."

Brian put on the shirt. He followed Miss Red Moon outside. The sun was setting.

"This is the dance," she said. She made a slow circle, lifting first her left foot and then her right. "Do as I do. When you finish, stretch your arms toward the sun. Then sing your desire."

"What shall I sing?" asked Brian.

"My song was about my grandfather," said Miss Red Moon. "I sang, 'I will meet my grandfather.'"

"My song will be 'I will meet my father,'" said Brian.

Brian and the woman danced in the circle. He stretched his arms out to the setting sun. Then he sang in a shrill high voice, "I will meet my father! He who left to do me honor! I will meet my father, who never came back!"

The yellow dog howled. Bob Boyd's spirit stepped out of the tall grass, revealing not only his face this time, but his whole form. A tall, strong-looking soldier in a blue uniform and a buffalo coat. Brian's heart beat as his father walked toward him. His anger at his father for leaving all those years ago melted into joy as he met him for the very first time.

The ghost walked up and smiled. "Howdy, son," he said, "I've been wanting to say hello."

"Howdy," said Brian. He touched his father's strong, warm hand. He had always imagined that ghosts were cold things, but Bob Boyd's ghost wasn't. "I never thought I'd get to see you," Brian said.

The ghost knelt down on the ground. "Climb on my shoulders," he said. "I want to show you something."

Brian climbed on his father's shoulders and the ghost of the tall man stood up. The boy turned for a moment. The house and Miss Red Moon seemed lost in a haze. Brian thought about Eliza and how she needed him.

"Don't worry," said the ghost in a soothing voice. "We won't be gone long."

Leaving behind his mother and his neighbor and the howl of the yellow dog, Brian rode the prairie on his father's shoulders. A faint light rose from his father's body when the sun set. The chill wind picked up, but Brian didn't feel it.

"Where are we going?" Brian asked his father.

"To a tree I know about," replied the ghost.

They walked over one grassy knoll after another. Darkness came and faded into dawn. At the top of one hill, they finally stopped. Sticking up in the distance was a lone cottonwood tree.

"Get down," said Brian's father.

Brian slid off his father's back and followed him as he walked toward the tree. In the side of the tree's trunk there was a big hole and all around it bees were buzzing. Brian's father walked up to the tree and stuck his hand into the hole. When he pulled his arm out, bees were stuck to it. And in his hand was a big piece of honeycomb. He gave Brian a piece and the boy ate it.

"Sweet, isn't it?" said the ghost. "Honey is one thing I miss most in death." He pointed to the tree trunk. "Now you. . . ," he said.

Brian thought of the ghost dancer doll in his pocket. He looked into his ghost father's eyes. It was as if he could look into them and straight through them at the same time. The boy walked up to the tree and stuck his arm into the hole.

"Reach deeper," the ghost instructed.

Brian did as he was told and felt something hard.

"Pull it out," said his father.

Brian grabbed the hard thing inside the tree trunk and pulled on it. His arm was covered with honey and bees, but he felt no stings. When he took his hand out of the hole, he was holding a sack.

The ghost knelt down. "Now you must go home," he whispered. Brian felt the spirit's warm breath on his face. A fragrance like burnt pine floated off his coat. "Give this sack to your mother," the ghost instructed. "Tell her I kept my promise."

Holding the sack against his chest, Brian rode on his ghost father's shoulders until they reached home. Brian slipped down onto the earth. The ghost leaned down with him and kissed the boy on his cheek. "I left you, but only because I wanted to do you honor," whispered Bob Boyd. "Remember me. . . ." Then he laid the buffalo coat on Brian's shoulders.

The boy ran inside the house, where Eliza and Miss Red Moon were waiting. Eliza was all well and standing at the stove, while Miss Red Moon sat at the table drinking coffee. The yellow dog ran up to Brian barking.

"Where have you been, boy?" said Eliza. She touched the sleeve of Brian's white ghost dancer shirt and the buffalo coat on his shoulders. She saw the honey on his face and hands. "What is all this?" she scolded. "What have you been up to?"

Brian looked at Miss Red Moon. "Did you tell her?"

Miss Red Moon's eyes twinkled. "How could I, when

I don't rightly know what happened? One minute you were there, the next you were gone."

"You mean you didn't see him?" said Brian.

Eliza put her hands on her hips. "See who? Will somebody speak English?"

Brian hugged his mother around her waist and told her all that had happened, and then he gave her the sack. When Eliza opened the sack, they saw that it was filled with gold! Tears streamed out of her eyes. "He said he would always take care of us. He kept his promise."

With the small fortune inside the sack, Brian and Eliza were comfortable for the rest of their days. They shared their wealth with Sallie Red Moon and took care of her in her old age. As for Bob Boyd's buffalo coat, it was handed down to Brian's children, as was the ghost dancer doll. And then there were the stories told over and over about a Buffalo Soldier's honor and the generous Lakota woman who had taught the soldier's son how to dance for a ghost.

> **Ghost Dance religion**—Nineteenth-century religion practiced by the Lakota (also known as the Sioux), Paiute, and other Native American nations.
> **Buffalo Soldiers**—African-American cavalry and infantry units, named for the buffalo coats they wore.

Tale of the Golden Ball

In the old times there was a beautiful little girl named Omara—beautiful to look at and beautiful in her ways. She lived in a small cottage with her mama and papa, on a poor plot of earth that bore few crops. Omara and her mother were happy. They were poor, but they had each other. And in spite of the stony soil, the woman of the house grew wonderful flowers. But the man of the house was bitter. Day after day, he cursed his luck because, instead of rich soil, his plough and hoe struck rock. Struggle made him mean and stingy and blind to the great treasure he did have—his family.

One day an old beggar man came along. Omara spied the beggar out of the window. Ragged as a sheet caught on a nail in the wind, he walked down the dusty road. This beggar was a bone, he was so skinny. But his walk was spry enough.

The beggar man knocked on the front door. Omara's father went to open it. Omara, who was quite shy, ran into the bedroom. Omara's mother stayed put by the table.

"What do you want?" Omara's father asked the beggar man.

"I'm monstrous hungry," the beggar said, stooping way over. "Got a hunk of bread for me?"

"Got a hunk for myself," said the father.

"Oh, give the old beggar a piece of bread," Omara's mother called out. She brought the beggar a piece of corn pone. The beggar man grabbed the bread and gobbled it up.

Inside the back room, Omara sneezed. The beggar took the chance to shuffle inside a bit.

"What's that I hear in the bedroom?" he asked. "Is that a mouse?"

"None of your business," Papa said.

"That's our daughter," said Mama. "She's in the other room."

"Does her hair shine like gold?" asked the beggar.

Papa laughed a bitter laugh. "What would we be doing with a gold-haired girl?" he said.

"Gold brings good luck," said the beggar man.

"Well, we got no gold," said Papa, "and we got no luck. And our daughter's hair is black. She's just ordinary."

"No such thing," said Mama. "My Omara's not ordinary. Her black hair is beautiful. And her skin glistens like a dark stone under water. And she's got beautiful ways about her."

"Hush up, woman," said Papa. "Our girl is ordinary. Ordinary, just like us."

Inside the bedroom, Omara was listening. She peeked

out of the room. She saw the beggar man curl his head around the corner, trying to look at her.

"Oh, my," sighed the beggar, "wouldn't it be good to get off my feet for a spell?"

"Go rest under a stone," said Papa.

"No, come sit by the fire," Mama offered. She pulled up a stool to the fire and the beggar sat down.

"This feels mighty good," said the old man. He stretched his arms out and they seemed much longer. He pointed to the mantel. "What would be even better is a whiff of tobacco," he said.

"I gave you something to eat," Papa grumbled. "You're sitting by my fire. Now you want to smoke my tobacco?"

"Give him a whiff," Mama said. "He probably ain't had a whiff from a pipe in a long time."

So, Papa filled his pipe with tobacco and handed it over to the beggar man.

The beggar man sat up much taller. "Now, give me a fire coal," he commanded.

"Who are you talking to like that?" Papa said.

The beggar man stood up. His stooped body was stretching out. He was twice the height he'd been when he'd knocked at the door.

"Give him what he wants," Omara's Mama said quickly.

Papa picked up a burning coal from the hearth in a little shovel. The beggar man reached over and picked it up in his bare hand and lit the pipe with it. Out of sight, Omara was watching.

Papa pushed Mama out of the way. The beggar man grinned. He was smoking the pipe all right and seemed to be enjoying it. But he was still holding the red hot coal in his other hand.

Omara let out a little cry.

"Oh, there's your pretty daughter," said the ragged man. He peeked inside the bedroom and Omara ran out.

The beggar man laughed and put the hot coal in his mouth. Mama and Papa stared in amazement. Omara hid behind Mama's skirt.

"I can see you ain't no ordinary beggar," Papa told the old man. "I can see that you got powers. We gave you something to eat. Now you do something for us."

"What would you like?" asked the old man.

"Give me some gold," said Omara's father. "Give me some luck."

"Very well," said the beggar man. "Let your daughter come here and take this little ball from me."

"What ball are you talking about?" said Papa.

The beggar spit something small, round, and gleaming into the air. "This here ball," he said.

Papa ran to catch the ball, but the beggar man caught it first.

"Is it gold?" Papa asked, peering into the man's hand.

The little ball shone like the sun.

"It looks like gold," said Mama.

"It's a golden ball," said the beggar man. "I'm going to give it to your daughter."

The old man put the ball on a string he took out of

his pocket and tied the string into a tight knot. Omara's Papa pushed her forward. The beggar put the golden ball around her neck. And in that instant, Omara's dark skin and hair turned golden.

Papa gasped. Omara looked at her hand. It looked as if she had a golden glove on. Mama threw herself at the beggar and beat him on the chest. "What have you done with our daughter?" she cried. "Change her back!"

The beggar man laughed a bitter laugh. He tipped his hat to Papa. "In payment for your generosity," he said, "your daughter is no longer ordinary. You now have gold in your house. You now have luck."

The beggar slipped through the house and ran out the back door. Omara's mama ran after him. "Come back!" she cried into the wind. The man ran down the road. Omara's mother ran too, but the old beggar man ran faster, vanishing into the dusk. Mama came home out of breath and alone.

Golden Omara sat in the middle of the floor. Golden tears ran out of her eyes, onto her golden cheeks. Meanwhile, Papa sat at the table, eating his corn pone.

"How can you sit there and eat?" said Mama. "When that old man has robbed your daughter?"

Papa grinned. "That beggar was a good conjurer, no doubt. We were lucky that he stopped by."

"Lucky?" said Mama. "You're either crazy or a fool!"

"Didn't he give Omara a solid gold charm?" Papa argued.

"An evil charm," said Mama. "That conjurer stole her beautiful skin, her beautiful hair."

"Hush up," said Papa. "Didn't you hear the man? Gold is the color of riches, the color of luck."

"Black is a rich color too," said Mama. She sat down on the floor with Omara. "You surely don't know what real riches are."

Mama wiped Omara's golden tears and kissed her golden cheek. "Don't cry, baby," she said, "I'm going to fix this."

Papa stood up. "What are you going to do?"

Mama grabbed the string on her daughter's neck. "What do you think?"

Papa raised his hand. "Don't you touch it! Our luck is in that golden ball! Leave it be!"

"Get away from me, man," said Mama, "this is my daughter!" She tried to break the string with her hand. But she couldn't. Then she tried to lift the golden ball from around Omara's neck. But as she lifted it, the string got smaller—so small that it wouldn't fit over the child's head.

"You see," said Papa. "The golden ball is magic. It won't come off anyway."

Omara started to cry.

"I'll cut it off," said Mama, getting a knife.

Omara bent her head forward while Mama cut at the string. But no amount of cutting would break it.

"Maybe the knife is too dull," said Mama.

"Or maybe that golden ball is meant to stay," said Papa.

Mama sharpened the knife and tried again. But no

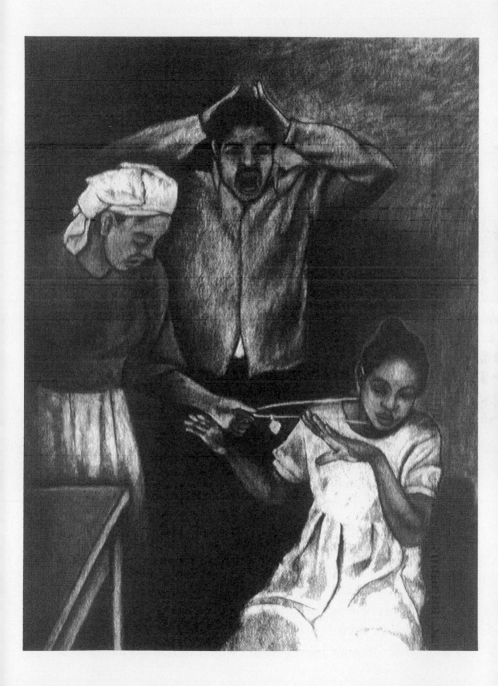

amount of cutting or yanking would help. Mama began to cry and Omara hugged her.

"Don't cry, Mama," said Omara. "I'm gold, but I'm the same everywhere else."

Mama kissed her daughter. "Yes," she said. "No one can ever steal your beautiful ways."

"Stop your whining," said Papa. "This is a good day. Our luck's going to change." He looked at Omara. "We got a piece of gold in the house."

Still the luck of the family didn't get better. It got worse. That spring Omara's mama passed away. She had tried and tried to get the golden charm from around her child's neck. She died of a broken heart, because she had failed.

"Forgive me," she said to Omara. "My love for you is strong. But not strong enough to break this spell. Do not forget that you were born beautiful. When you look at the flowers I planted, remember who you are."

Papa buried Mama next to the flower garden. Sadness filled the corners of the house. Day after day Papa cursed his fate and the stony soil. Then one day he said to Omara, "Maybe I should start a business. Maybe then our luck will change. And it might be our luck will change if I show you off to the world."

Omara bowed her head. She didn't want to show off. She was still shy and hadn't seen many other people. In fact, since the beggar man had given her the golden ball, she hadn't seen a soul outside her family.

But Omara's papa had his way. He started a furniture

business. He made chairs and tables out of twigs from the forest. Omara was to sit outside, selling the furniture.

Omara's job wasn't easy. Not too many folks lived around that way. And those that did come by thought that Omara looked funny. There were no other golden people in those parts.

"Who's that strange-looking person with the golden skin?" people would say. One mean boy even went so far as to throw rocks at her. Omara ran into the woods crying.

"Gold isn't lucky," Omara said. "I'm gold, but nobody likes me. I hate this golden ball."

"Don't talk about the charm in that way," said Papa. "You're the one who must be doing something wrong. Everybody knows that gold is lucky. You just have to give the charm a chance to work—that's all."

So day after day Omara sat outside, selling furniture. And in the evening, she walked among the flowers in her mother's garden. In the years that followed, many people got to know her and Omara became less shy. And more and more folks began to buy the furniture. After a while, Papa was a lot richer.

"Told you our luck would change," he said to Omara. "Your mama didn't believe in the golden ball, but I do." He touched the string around Omara's neck. "You just make sure you don't tell anybody about our good luck charm. They might try to steal it and I'll have to kill them."

A shiver ran down Omara's spine. "All right," she said.

An old woman came to buy a chair. "Guess you never bought a chair from a girl with a golden face," boasted Papa.

"The girl's face is fine enough," said the woman, "but I bought the chair because I liked the way she talked to me."

An old man bought a stool. "Did you see my girl's gold hair?" said Papa. "Is that what made you stop and buy that stool?"

"I heard your daughter was honest," said the old man. "That's why I came by. I bought the stool from her because I needed it."

A young man stopped by and bought many things. He wanted Omara to tell him about every piece.

"I think you and your papa must be rich," he said.

She smiled sadly. "Rich in some ways."

"My girl sure knows how to sell some furniture," Papa boasted to the young man. "Guess she charmed you with her golden eyes."

"I do like the color gold," the young man confessed. "I'd like to marry Omara."

Papa agreed, so Omara had a fiancé. But before Omara got married, Papa got married himself. According to what folks said, Papa's new wife knew about charms, because she was a conjure woman.

Omara's new stepmother was sly and greedy. She loved spending the money that Papa and Omara made. But Omara also noticed her stepmother eyeing the golden ball.

"It's a charm," she blurted out to the conjure woman.

Even though her father had warned her not to, something inside made her speak. "You might as well know that the golden ball is what made us rich."

"Do you wear it in your sleep?" asked the stepmother.

Omara sighed. "I have to. It won't come off."

The stepmother came closer. "Have you tried to take it off?"

Omara smiled her sad smile. "My mother tried and failed. So I'm sure I'm not strong enough. And Papa says he'll kill the person who tries to take it off." She looked at her stepmother. "But maybe somebody who knows about charms could get it off, anyway. Maybe somebody who knows about charms might have a magic knife or some magic scissors."

The very next morning, when Omara was in the flower garden, her stepmother crept up behind her. As she knelt over the flowers, Omara could feel the woman's presence. She could also see her shadow. Her stepmother had a strange-looking pair of scissors in her hand. Omara guessed what was happening. Her greedy stepmother wanted the golden ball. Omara bowed her head and pretended not to see or hear her. Kneeling perfectly still, she felt the cold touch of the scissors on her neck. And with a snip, she felt the string slip away as the golden ball tumbled into the grass.

Omara turned quickly to see her stepmother. The conjure woman was on her hands and knees, searching the ground.

"You'd better not tell your father!" the woman hissed, pointing the strange-looking scissors at Omara.

Omara ran away. She was glad to be rid of the charm. It felt as if a heavy chain was off her neck. Her feet lifted off the ground as she ran to the spring. Her body felt fluttery, as if she were being kissed by butterflies. When she got to the spring, she looked at her reflection and started to laugh.

It's me! she thought. *My hair! My face! My arms, my feet!* She splashed her feet in the spring. Then she washed her black hair and her face, which glistened like a dark stone under water. She let water from the stream trickle over her arms and shoulders. Then she looked up to see her father and stepmother watching her.

"Who are you?" Papa asked.

Omara stood up. Her skin was wet and her clothes were mud-splattered. She smiled. "Don't you know me, Papa?"

He looked at her long and hard, as if he were trying to remember something.

She took his hand. "It's me," she said, "Omara."

Papa snatched his hand away. "My Omara is golden," he said. "She wears a golden ball." He looked at his wife. "Where is my daughter anyway?"

"I haven't seen her," said the stepmother. She pointed at Omara. "Maybe this strange girl killed her."

Omara's father shook Omara by the shoulders. "What have you done to my daughter?" he shouted.

"I am your daughter," she said.

"What have you done with the golden charm she wore on her neck?" Papa demanded.

Omara pointed at her stepmother. "Ask your wife."

Papa turned to his wife. "Well? What do you know about it?"

"Not a thing," Omara's stepmother declared. "I do know that there is a stranger in our yard and that your daughter is missing."

Omara's fiancé came to call. "Where is Omara?" he asked.

Omara ran up to him. "Don't you know me?"

Omara's fiancé pushed her away. "You have Omara's sweet voice. But the Omara I love is rich. My Omara doesn't wear muddy clothes."

"I am your Omara," she said, "please believe me. Let me tell you my story."

"I wouldn't believe a story coming from you," said her fiancé.

"You shouldn't believe her," shouted the stepmother. "Omara is dead! And that one in the muddy dress is the one who killed her!"

Other people came by to witness the scene. "My daughter has been murdered," cried Omara's papa. "And the charm she wore around her neck has been stolen!"

"Who did it?" one of the crowd asked.

The stepmother pointed at Omara again. "That one!"

Omara ran and the crowd chased her. She ran into the garden and stumbled. Sitting on a rock was an old beggar man. The same old beggar who'd come to the family's home, all those years ago.

The beggar stood up. "Wait!" he shouted. He waved his arms at the crowd. In one hand he held up something small and gleaming. "Here is the charm," he announced.

Omara's papa leapt forward. "Give it to me!" he said. "Where did you find it?"

The beggar closed his hand around the golden ball. "I found it here," he said, "in the grass." The beggar looked at Omara's stepmother. The woman looked away and backed off. The beggar man took a string out of his pocket and put the golden ball on it. Then he stepped up to Omara and put the string around Omara's neck.

"And this young woman is no murderer," said the beggar. "She is Omara."

Omara's father drew in a breath. Omara began to weep. With the charm around her neck, once more she was golden.

The beggar man told the crowd the whole story. How he'd given Omara's family the golden ball.

Omara's father came up to her and said, "I'm sorry, daughter."

Omara stood up. She bowed her head and lifted her hands to touch the string on her neck. She had never tried herself to take the charm off. She had always thought that she wasn't strong enough. She had always been afraid of her father.

She looked at her mother's flowers. The flowers gazed back with velvet-dark eyes. Omara took a deep breath. She felt the strength of her mother's love rise up from the earth. Then she felt the strength of her own feet and legs and heart. She put that strength into her hands and lifted the charm off. Tears rolled down her cheeks, tears of joy that were no longer golden. Clutching the charm in her dark hand, she faced the crowd proudly.

"I am Omara," she said. She looked at them. Goodness poured out of her eyes.

"How beautiful she is!" said a man in the crowd. "She stands like a queen."

Omara's father bowed his head. In Omara he recognized the grace of his first wife. "How could I have forgotten my greatest treasure?" he said, offering his arm to Omara. "Come home with me, daughter."

"You did not know me," said Omara. "You of all people should have known me. I cannot come home with you."

"Then come home with me," said Omara's fiancé. "Now that I see who you really are, you can be my wife. Since you're Omara, I'm sure you won't be wearing muddy dresses anymore. Why don't you marry me?"

"I won't marry you," said Omara. "You didn't believe in me."

The beggar man stepped up. "I'm the one you should go with. I was under a spell. I could only be free myself when you discovered that removing the golden ball was in your own power." The little beggar man stood up tall. He became young and handsome. His ragged clothes transformed into richly textured and bright-colored garments. He offered his arm to Omara.

"You are my queen," he said. "I will give you a crown for your shining dark hair."

Omara smiled as her splattered clothes changed into

rich garments too. But she turned away from the beggar man.

"Keep your crown," she told him. "My family was generous to you. Yet you repaid us by robbing me. My mother died of a broken heart because of you."

Omara walked away from the crowd, leaving them all behind.

"Wait!" cried Omara's father.

Omara turned and tossed the golden ball into the air. Her stepmother ran to catch it. But the charm kept spinning. The young man who was no longer a beggar tried to catch it too, as did Omara's fiancé. But Omara had taken good aim. The ball landed in her father's wide-open mouth. As he waved good-bye, he was turning golden.

Omara didn't look back. She walked toward the hill. As she got closer, the side of the hill opened, revealing a world of cheerful sun and comforting shade. A world with people in many-colored clothing. People who welcomed her with their smiles.

Akiba's Singing Water

A kiba Yaeger was eleven years old when she met one of the spirits of Singing Creek. All her life she'd been standing on the back porch listening. Listening to the twisting water below.

"What are you doing, child?" asked Grandfather.

"Oh, nothing," said Akiba, "just listening."

Grandfather was quiet a minute. Sunlight bounced on the water. "Well, I'm listening, too," he said, "but I don't hear anything."

"Don't you hear it?" Akiba said, closing her eyes. "Don't you hear the song in the water?"

Grandfather shoved Akiba's schoolbooks into her hands. "I don't hear nothing," he said, "because there's nothing to hear. That song in the creek business is just an old tale."

"But I can hear it in my ear," argued Akiba.

Grandfather lifted an eyebrow. "Well, since you're so smart, just what is the song the creek is singing?"

Akiba shrugged. "I can't make out the words. All

that I hear is *burble, burble.* But I know folks are singing in there."

Akiba walked to school along the marshy path. She stood by a tree and looked down at the creek. The old tale that Grandfather mentioned is a sad one:

There be these people long ago, called Ibo. They brought here to be somebody's slaves. But they didn't be nobody's slaves. When they get off the boat, they turn around and walk straight into the water. When they walk into the water, they be singing. Couldn't nobody stop them. They walk right into the deep part, until all their heads disappear. Folks say they be drowned. But if they be drowned, how come there's singing in the water?

One night the singing in the water was so loud. Grandfather heard nothing. He was snoring in his bed. But Akiba heard, even over Grandfather's noises. She got dressed and went out onto the porch. The porch was lit by moonlight. She walked down the stairs and whispered:

"What are you singing, creek?"

The creek's sounds got louder. But all Akiba could make out was *burble, burble.*

Akiba walked down the path in her bare feet. Her toes sank into the mud. *If I had me a boat,* she thought, *I could get out to the middle.* But there wasn't a boat around. Lying next to the creek bank was Grandfather's old bucket.

Akiba dipped the bucket into the creek and filled it with dark water. Then she leaned over the bucket and listened. A small spotted snake twisted up out of the bucket and stared at her.

"Silly Akiba," said the snake, "you cannot capture the song of hundreds in one small bucket."

Akiba backed away. "How come you can talk?" she cried.

"Because I came out of the creek," the snake explained. "That creek is all voices."

Akiba stood up. "I hear them," she said, "but I can't understand what they're singing."

"Toss the bucket into the water," said the snake.

"It's my grandfather's bucket," said Akiba.

"If you want to know the song," said the snake, "you must do as I say."

Akiba tossed the bucket into the creek. It floated away with the snake into the shadows.

"Where are you?" asked Akiba. "What happened to the bucket?"

"Over here," a voice replied. A long boat floated out of the shadows. A boy hung on to the side of it.

"What are you waiting for?" the boy said. "Come with me!" The boy had the voice of the snake.

A breeze playing on the water whipped at Akiba's dress. "Where are you going?" she asked.

"For a ride," said the boy. "In order to really hear the song, we have to go out some." He climbed into the boat and beckoned to her.

Akiba's skin felt shivery as she waded in to her ankles. The water swirled around her and came up to her waist. She remembered the old tale about the folks drowning. The boy paddled the boat closer and she grabbed hold of it.

"Get in," he said.

Akiba got in and he gave her a paddle.

"We are going to the deepest part," he said, "to the drop that takes you out to the ocean."

Akiba felt frightened. "Who are you?" she asked.

The boy looked over his shoulder. Something in his eyes was like the small snake's. "Don't you know me?" he said with a laugh. "You caught me in an old bucket."

Akiba looked down into the twisting creek. What a fool she'd been to get into the boat. She put her hand into the cold water and thought about jumping. The boy touched her.

"I am not here to harm you," he said, "but to teach you. I am your ancestor."

"My ancestor?" said Akiba. "But you're not that much older than I am."

The boy continued to paddle. "I am fixed in time," he said, "never to grow a day older. I am one of those who walked into the water."

"One of the Ibo people?" whispered Akiba.

"Yes," said the boy. "I was out fishing with my grandfather, my father, and brothers. My mother and two sisters were washing. My grandmother sat stirring a clay pot of bitter leaf soup. Some people came and took us all away. They surprised us and we were outnumbered. They took away most of my village."

"Couldn't you fight back?" asked Akiba.

"We tried," said the boy. "But in the end, we were captured. We were chained inside a long boat and brought here."

The boat stopped at a place that was perfectly still.

"They thought that we drowned," the boy said, turning around. "But we didn't."

"What happened then?" asked Akiba.

"On the journey over, my grandfather grew a snake inside his belly. When we got off of the boat, the snake inside my grandfather started to sing. My grandfather sang with the snake and my father sang with my grandfather. Then we all started singing. The song of the snake said to go home."

"You swam all the way?" said Akiba.

"When our heads disappeared under the water," the boy explained, "the snake swam out of my grandfather's mouth. My grandfather hung on to its tail, because it was a magic snake. My grandfather knew that. Grandmother held on to Grandfather. Then my father held on to her. I took my father's hand and then my mother's. My sister held my mother's hand and then my brother's. Our whole village held on to each other. And we swam. We swam all the way home—until we touched the coast of Africa."

Akiba looked out. "You were strong."

"We are proud and we had come too far," said the boy. "Besides, beneath the ocean, there is a swift river. It takes no time at all to get home, if you know the right route."

Moonlight was on the boat. The creek was a still pool above the drop to the ocean. But the voices of the creek swirled up all around them.

"I can hear the song!" said Akiba. "But the words
. . . I don't understand them."

"They are in a language you have forgotten," the boy
told her.

"Will you teach me the song in my language?" she
asked him.

The boy came closer. Akiba touched his arm. He
whispered in her ear. There was a big smile on her face.

"Now you must sing that song," he said. "Sing so
that the whole world will hear."

Akiba laughed. "I don't think that my voice is loud
enough."

The boy smiled. "Maybe I'll give you a present to
help out."

Akiba held out her hand. "I like presents."

"Not now," said the boy. "Tomorrow." He turned
away from Akiba and gazed into the creek. "I am going
home," he said. "Would you like to come with me? You
are a special girl. I heard your whisper all the way across
the ocean."

"Is that why you came here?" asked Akiba.

"Yes," said the boy. "I decided to pay you a visit. I let
you catch me in your bucket." He turned to her again.
"Would you like to come home with me?"

Akiba closed her eyes and listened.

"Still listening to the creek?" asked the boy.

"No," said Akiba, opening her eyes again. "I am listening to my grandfather snoring. He's at home, too—
my home. If I go with you, he will miss me."

"Then, good-bye," said the boy. "Sing your song. I

will be listening." He kissed Akiba on the cheek and jumped into the water.

Akiba paddled toward home. As she dipped her paddle in and out, the creek voices became stronger. They were the voices of young women and of children, of old men, of aunts and of uncles, of boys and of grandfathers. Akiba smiled, because she understood their song.

At the bend in the creek, she waded into the water. She pushed the lovely boat toward shore. When the boat touched the bank, it was no longer a boat, but Grandfather's old bucket. Akiba picked up the bucket and ran to the house. There were still stars in the sky. *Maybe I'm dreaming,* she thought. Leaving the bucket on the porch, she slipped inside. Grandfather was still asleep in his bed—snoring.

The next morning, Grandfather woke Akiba up.

"Get up, lazy girl," he said, shaking her arm. "And why are you asleep in your school clothes?"

Akiba rubbed her face. "Sorry," she said, "I was tired last night." Grandfather went to fix breakfast, while Akiba changed her clothes. The hem of the dress she had been wearing was wet. When she sat down to eat, Grandfather went out onto the porch.

"Come here!" he called out suddenly. "Come see what somebody left us!"

Akiba ran outside. Where she had left the old bucket, there was a drum.

"Look," said Grandfather, "a beautiful drum!" He picked the drum up and held it out to her.

"Thank you," Akiba said. "I think this is mine."

She felt the smooth hide of the drum's top. She felt the carved snake on its side.

Grandfather shook his head in wonder. "Who could have left such a wonderful present?" he asked.

Akiba looked down at the twisting creek, where sunlight was bouncing. She listened to the creek's song. Then she began to sing and play her new drum. Then she was quiet again, listening.

Grandfather's eyes lit up. He looked down at the creek. "I hear it," he said. "At last I do believe I hear it."

> Miri me come
> Miri me go
> Water carry me here
> Water carry me home
>
> Feet carry me home
> Legs carry me home
> Arms carry me home
> Neck carry me home
>
> Miri me come
> Miri me go
> Water carry me here
> Water carry me home
>
> Mouth carry me home
> Nose carry me home
> Eyes carry me home
> Head carry me home

Miri me come
Miri me go
Water carry me here
Water carry me home

Father carry me home
Mother carry me home
Sister carry me home
Brother carry me home

Miri me come
Miri me go
We live!
Do not forget us!

Water carry me here
Water carry me home

Heart carry me home
Voice carry me home
God carry me home
Song carry me home

Miri carry me here
Miri carry me home!

Miri—A word for water in the Ibo language.

About the Stories

"Vampire Bugs" is based on "Bugs," a folk tale recorded by Mary Alicia Owen in her book *Voodoo Tales as Told Among the Negroes of the Old Southwest*, published in 1893. Ms. Owen lived in St. Louis, Missouri, and was a member of the American Folk-lore Society.

"Little Mose" is an adaptation of the Charles Waddell Chesnutt story "Sis Becky's Pickaniny," which appeared in his collection *The Conjure Woman*, published in 1899. Mr. Chestnutt, a prolific writer, was the first African-American to receive serious attention for his stories and novels. Set in North Carolina, Mr. Chesnutt's story was told largely in African-American dialect, by an old man named Julius who served as narrator. I have retold the tale from the point of view of Mose, the child in the story.

"The Voodoo Queen" is a fiction story inspired by the legendary life of nineteenth-century voodoo queen Marie Laveau. In actuality, "Madame L.," as she was often called, had not one but fifteen children. But one of these, a daughter bearing her name, succeeded her as queen.

Unaware that there were two Maries, some people assumed that the mother and the daughter were one and the same person—a woman who lived to be nearly a hundred but who never appeared to grow old.

"Ghost Dancer" is a fiction story inspired by the Native American Ghost Dance religion, popular among the Sioux (Lakota), Paiute, and other nations in the last half of the nineteenth century. The words "You shall see your grandfather" appear in one of the ceremonial Sioux Ghost Dance songs recorded by ethnologist James Mooney.

"Tale of the Golden Ball" is an adaptation of Mary Alicia Owen's "De Tale ob de Gol'en Ball," which appears in *Voodoo Tales as Told Among the Negroes of the Old Southwest*.

"Akiba's Singing Water" is a fiction story inspired by the legend of a mass suicide of Ibo people captured for slaves, taking place at Dunbar Creek on St. Simons, one of the Georgia Sea Islands.

Bibliography

* Books for Young Readers

Arthur, Stanley. *Old New Orleans*. Pelican Publishing Co., 1990.

Asbury, Herbert. *The French Quarter: An Informal History of the New Orleans Underworld*. Alfred A. Knopf, 1936.

Brown, Dee. *Bury My Heart at Wounded Knee*. Holt, Rinehart & Winston, 1970.

Bull, John, and Farrand, John, Jr., American Museum of Natural History. *The Audubon Society Field Guide to North American Birds, Eastern Region*. Alfred A. Knopf, 1977.

Chesnutt, Charles W. *The Conjure Woman*. Houghton Mifflin Co., Riverside Press, 1899.

deLavigne, Jeanne. *Ghost Stories of Old New Orleans*. Rinehart & Co., 1946.

Dorson, Richard M. *Negro Tales from Pine Bluff, Arkansas, and Calvin, Michigan*. Indiana University Press, 1958.

*Downey, Fairfax Davis. *The Buffalo Soldiers in the Indian Wars*. McGraw-Hill Book Co., 1969.

Estés, Clarissa Pinkola. *Women Who Run with the Wolves: Myths and Stories of the Wild Woman Archetype*. Ballantine Books, 1992.

*Fairman, Tony. *Bury My Bones but Keep My Words*. Henry Holt & Co., 1991.

"Folk-Lore Scrap-book," in *Journal of American Folk-lore*, vol. 7, pp. 66–67. Houghton Mifflin Co., 1894.

Fox, Carl, and Landshoff, H. *The Doll*. Harry N. Abrams, 1973.

Freeney, Mildred, and Henry, Mary T. *A List of Manuscripts, Published Works and Related Items in the Charles Waddell Chesnutt Collection of the Erastus Milo Cravath Memorial Library*. Fisk University, 1954.

"Ghost Dance at Pine Ridge," in *Journal of American Folk-lore*, vol. 4, pp. 160–61, 1891.

*Goss, Linda, and Barnes, Marian E. *Talk That Talk*. Simon & Schuster, 1989.

*Hamilton, Virginia. *The Dark Way: Stories from the Spirit World*. Harcourt Brace Jovanovich, 1990.

————. *The People Could Fly: American Black Folktales*. Alfred A. Knopf, 1985.

Hart, Mickey, and Stevens, Jay. *Drumming at the Edge of Magic: a Journey into the Spirit of Percussion*. Harper San Francisco, 1990.

Katz, William Loren. *Black Indians: A Hidden Heritage*. Atheneum, 1986.

*Lyons, Mary E. *Raw Head, Bloody Bones: African Tales of the Supernatural*. Charles Scribner's Sons, 1991.

Martine, Louis. *The New Orleans Voodoo Tarot*. Destiny Books, 1992.

*McKissack, Patricia C. *The Dark-Thirty: Southern Tales of the Supernatural*. Alfred A. Knopf, 1992.

Mooney, James. *The Ghost-Dance Religion and the Sioux Outbreak of 1890, Introduction to the Bison Book Edition by Raymond J. DeMalkie*. University of Nebraska Press, 1991. Originally published: Washington, D.C., GPO, 1896, as part 2 of the fourteenth report of the Bureau of Ethnology, 1892–93.

*Osborne, Mary Pope. *American Tall Tales*. Alfred A. Knopf, 1991.

―――. *Mermaid Tales from Around the World*. Scholastic, 1993.

Owen, Mary Alicia. *Voodoo Tales as Told Among the Negroes of the Old Southwest*. G. P. Putnam's Sons, 1893.

Porter, Kenneth W. "A Legend of the Biloxi," in *Journal of American Folk-lore*, vol. 59, pp. 168–73, 1946.

Review of *Old Rabbit the Voodoo and Other Sorcerers*, in *Journal of American Folk-lore*, vol. 6, pp. 161–62, 1893.

Rigaud, Milo. *Secrets of Voodoo*. Translated from the French by Robert B. Cross. City Lights Books, 1969.

"St. Simons and Sea Island Georgia"—a pamphlet issued by St. Simons Island Chamber of Commerce and Visitors Center.

*San Souci, Robert D. *Short and Shivery: Thirty Chilling Tales*. Delacorte Press, 1987.

Saxon, Lyle. *Fabulous New Orleans*. Century Co., 1928.

"Superstitions of Negroes in New Orleans," in *Journal of American Folk-lore*, vol. 5, pp. 330–32, 1892.

Tallant, Robert. *Voodoo in New Orleans*. Collier Books, 1946.

Utley, Robert, J. *Last Days of the Sioux Nation*. Yale University Press, 1963.

About the Author

Following the oral tradition of African-American storytellers, Sharon Dennis Wyeth weaves a collection resonant with voices of the past and her own. Taking on the cloak of conjurer, she has created a unique collection, both lyric and probing.

Sharon Dennis Wyeth's most recent novel for Delacorte Press was *The World of Daughter McGuire*. She has written many books for young readers, including *Always My Dad*, *Ginger Brown: Too Many Houses*, the Pen Pals series, and *Annie K.'s Theater*. She lives in Montclair, New Jersey, with her husband, Sims, and daughter, Georgia.

Curtis E. James has a B.F.A. and an M.F.A. from Pratt Institute in Brooklyn, New York. He now resides in New York City.